Dear Parent:

Your child's love of reading starts here!

Every child learns to read in a different way and at his or her own speed. Some go back and forth between reading levels and read favorite books again and again. Others read through each level in order. You can help your young reader improve and become more confident by encouraging his or her own interests and abilities. From books your child reads with you to the first books he or she reads alone, there are I Can Read Books for every stage of reading:

SHARED READING
Basic language, word repetition, and whimsical illustrations, ideal for sharing with your emergent reader

BEGINNING READING
Short sentences, familiar words, and simple concepts for children eager to read on their own

READING WITH HELP
Engaging stories, longer sentences, and language play for developing readers

READING ALONE
Complex plots, challenging vocabulary, and high-interest topics for the independent reader

I Can Read Books have introduced children to the joy of reading since 1957. Featuring award-winning authors and illustrators and a fabulous cast of beloved characters, I Can Read Books set the standard for beginning readers.

A lifetime of discovery begins with the magical words **"I Can Read!"**

Visit www.icanread.com for information
on enriching your child's reading experience.

The Adventures of Paddington: Paddington and the Pigeon

Based on the Paddington novels written and created by Michael Bond
PADDINGTON™ and PADDINGTON BEAR™ © Paddington and Company Limited/Studiocanal S.A.S 2020
Paddington Bear™, Paddington™ and PB™ are trademarks of Paddington and Company Limited
Licensed on behalf of Studiocanal S.A.S by Copyrights Group
www.paddington.com

Library of Congress Control Number: 2020933854

ISBN 978-0-06-298315-2 (trade bdg.) — ISBN 978-0-06-298314-5 (pbk.)

20 21 22 23 24 LSCC 10 9 8 7 6 5 4 3 2 1 ❖ First Edition

My First

SHARED READING

I Can Read!

The Adventures of
Paddington™
Paddington and the Pigeon

Based on the episode "Paddington and the Pigeon"
by Jon Foster and James Lamont

Adapted by Alyssa Satin Capucilli

HARPER
An Imprint of HarperCollinsPublishers

In this story you will meet:

Paddington: He loves his aunt Lucy and writes her lots of letters. He also loves sweet orange jam called marmalade.

The Brown Family: Mr. and Mrs. Brown, Judy, and Jonathan love having a bear at home.

Mrs. Bird: She looks after the Brown family. She can fix many things!

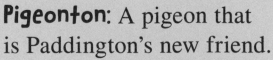

Pigeonton: A pigeon that is Paddington's new friend.

Dear Aunt Lucy,

Today I made a new friend!

We met him in a funny way . . .

Paddington was playing a game
with the Brown family.
Suddenly, there was
a loud noise!

Something had fallen
down the chimney.
What could it be?

"It's a pigeon,"
said Mr. Brown.

The pigeon sat very still.

He did not fly away.

The bird hopped onto the game.

He pecked at a small hat.

The hat landed on his head.

The hat made everyone smile!
"Hello, little fellow,"
said Paddington.
"Let's call you Pigeonton!"

Mrs. Brown and Paddington
looked at Pigeonton.

"I think his wing is hurt,"
said Paddington.
"What can we do?"

"I can fix the pigeon's wing,"
said Mrs. Bird.
"But he must rest, too."

"I will make a nest,"
said Paddington.
"He can rest in the nest."

"I will use sticks and glue,"
said Paddington.
"I will use feathers, too!"

Pigeonton loved his new nest.

Paddington loved taking
care of his new friend.
He showed Pigeonton
how to use a toothbrush.

Paddington showed Pigeonton yummy food, too!
"I put marmalade on everything," said Paddington.

Paddington took Pigeonton
for a walk.

Pigeonton looked at the sky.

"You will fly again soon,"
said Paddington.

At bedtime, Paddington tucked
Pigeonton into bed.
Sharing his room was fun!

One day, when Paddington
woke up, Pigeonton was gone!
Where was Pigeonton?

Then Paddington saw Pigeonton.

He was flying here and there.

"Come back to your nest,"
said Paddington.

"You must rest."

"Pigeonton's wing is fixed,"
said Mrs. Bird.

"He does not need to rest.
Pigeonton needs to be set free."

Paddington was sad,
but he knew what to do.
He opened the window wide.
Pigeonton flew high!
"I will miss you,"
said Paddington.

But that night,
there was a peck
at the window.
It was Pigeonton!

"You can visit anytime,"
called Paddington.

"Coo, coo!"

Pigeonton would be back soon!

It made me sad to say goodbye
to my friend, but I know
Pigeonton will visit again soon.

Love from Paddington